Ha

A Bekki the Beautician Cozy Mystery

Cindy Bell

Copyright © 2013 Cindy Bell

All rights reserved.

All rights reserved. No part of this publication may be reproduced or transmitted in any form or by any means, electronic or mechanical, including photocopy, recording, or any information storage or retrieval system, without permission in writing from the publisher.

This is a work of fiction. The characters, incidents and locations portrayed in this book and the names herein are fictitious. Any similarity to or identification with the locations, names, characters or history of any person, product or entity is entirely coincidental and unintentional.

All trademarks and brands referred to in this book are for illustrative purposes only, are the property of their respective owners and not affiliated with this publication in any way. Any trademarks are being used without permission, and the publication of the trademark is not authorized by, associated with or sponsored by the trademark owner.

ISBN-13: 978-1492938378

ISBN-10: 1492938378

More Cozy Mysteries by Cindy Bell

Heavenly Highland Inn Cozy Mystery Series

Murdering the Roses (Heavenly Highland Inn Cozy Mystery 1)

Bekki the Beautician Cozy Mystery Series

A Dyed Blonde and a Dead Body (Bekki the Beautician Cozy Mystery 2)

Mascara and Murder (Bekki the Beautician Cozy Mystery 3)

Pageant and Poison (Bekki the Beautician Cozy Mystery 4)

Table of Contents

Chapter One.. 1

Chapter Two 18

Chapter Three...29

Chapter Four..43

Chapter Five 63

Chapter Six 87

Chapter One

The rear view mirror did not reflect as much as she wished it would. Bekki carefully brushed a fingertip along the slope of her perfectly groomed eyebrow. She blinked her long lashes twice, loosening the grip of the mascara that had become a little too dried out in the summer heat. She tilted her head to catch a glimpse of her lipstick which was equally dried out. She quickly freshened it and then tucked the tube back into her purse. The purse was one of her most treasured items; the latest fashion trend to sweep through the city was big bags. This came as a relief to her, as the tiny little clutches of the year before had made it nearly impossible for her to carry everything that she needed.

She sat back in the driver's seat of her navy blue Ford Focus and started the engine. She had just stopped off at a gas station to refuel her gas tank and refill her stomach. With a bag of chips beside her and a cheeseburger wrapper already on the floorboard she was ready to get back on the road. As she drove off she recalled the grimace of annoyance that the woman behind the counter had given her when she ordered the greasy food along with a genuine sugar filled soda. Bekki didn't always eat fast food, but when she did, she enjoyed every bite. When she had the time she enjoyed cooking sumptuous meals full of fresh vegetables and fruits, paired perfectly with the finest cuts of meat. Despite that, she was slender, with a petite frame. When her friends discussed what new diet they were on, to look even more perfect than they already were, Bekki only shrugged and ate what she pleased. She couldn't imagine having to curb her appetite, as she had a big one.

As a popular beautician she always tried to look her best, but it was not a competition to Bekki. That was why she loved her job. She believed that every woman was not just beautiful, but absolutely stunning. When the right features were accented, and she saw that burst of confidence rise in a customer's eyes, she felt just as thrilled.

"Women are born beautiful, and will always be beautiful," she would smile as she shared their joy in the reflection of the mirror. "That's what my mother has always told me."

But no amount of makeup or fine clothing could change what had just become very ugly in Bekki's life. A week before she had caught her boyfriend of two years in their bed, with another woman. It was so shocking to Bekki that she almost didn't believe it despite the fact that she had seen it. She tried to convince herself that maybe he had been drugged, maybe he was being blackmailed, maybe he had temporary amnesia. When he finally managed to get his pants on, and the busty blonde he was with brushed past her in a rush to get out the door, Trevor didn't offer any of those explanations. In fact he didn't offer any explanation at all. He just shrugged in that indifferent way he had, which she had once thought made him intriguing.

"I'm just not a one woman kind of guy Bekki," he said as if it should be simple to comprehend. That dismissive attitude, that casual demeanor had been one of the first reasons she was attracted to him, but now that he was turning that detachment on her, she realized how much it could hurt.

"But I thought…" she started to say, still so shocked that it felt as if her tongue and lips had gone numb.

"What? We were going to get married, have babies?" he asked with a laugh as he fished a pack of cigarettes out of the pocket of his jeans. "I'm not interested in that kind of life Bekki, this isn't Harroway."

No, it certainly isn't, Bekki thought to herself as she felt her heart tear into shreds. There was no truth to it breaking, at least not in her case, it felt more like a chainsaw had been taken to it.

That night as she wept over the man she had thought Trevor was, and her frustration with herself for not seeing the truth beyond the flash of his smile and the gleam of his eyes, she kept hearing his words. "This isn't Harroway." Harroway was her home town. A tiny little place nestled in the middle of Connecticut. It still had quaint little shops, a town square, and even family owned businesses, one of which belonged to her family.

When Bekki moved to New York City she had been teased quite often by her friends about her small town heritage, especially by Trevor who considered himself the quintessential modern man at the forefront of fashion and technology. Bekki had been a little embarrassed by their comments, but in general she ignored them. She was very confident in herself, and could care less about anyone's criticism, but in that moment when Trevor acted as if she shouldn't even be surprised that he had been cheating on her, she felt like a small town fool. She decided it was time to go home to Harroway.

***

Halfway through her journey there she felt the ache return. Bekki was very smart, she could advise her friends about their relationships, offering inspiring comments of inner strength and refusing to settle. But none of those words meant a thing to her as the image of Trevor's dismissive smirk kept returning to her mind. Her once unshakable confidence and determination were a little damaged, and she was eager to return to the comfort of her family. Bekki had grown up in her mother's hair and beauty salon, Harroway's Hair & Beauty. It was the place to be for all of the women in the town, and so Bekki had in a way been raised by the entire community.

Everyone had an interest in her life and her future. Most of the women would show up with little gifts and trinkets for Bekki when she was little, and as she grew into a teenager they were all there to offer her their motherly advice about boys, college, and the big city. Bekki had missed that since she had been in New York City, but she hadn't missed everyone being in the middle of her business, and knowing everything about her. At least in New York she didn't have to worry about Mrs. Mueller bringing up that time she chopped her hair off to the scalp because she wanted a Mohawk.

The entire salon had been in uproar over that because they all marvelled over Bekki's thick, wavy, black hair. It paired well with her clear blue eyes, and accented her olive skin. She had cut it so short that in the end her mother gave in and gave her the Mohawk. She spent a gleeful summer as what she thought was the coolest kid in town.

She laughed a little as she remembered that and turned down the long highway that would take her to Harroway. She was leaving everything she had thought she wanted behind, but now that she was almost home, she couldn't help but wonder why she had ever left in the first place.

***

When she pulled into the driveway of her parents' house, she was stunned by how little it had changed. Of course she had been home to visit now and then, but she had expected it to seem smaller, or older, in some way. Instead it was the same off-white clapboard that it had been when she moved away. The front door swung open and her mother came rushing out. Her mother was a near reflection of Bekki, with the same thick, dark hair which she wore shorter, and the clear blue eyes that revealed every emotion that she felt. Bekki stepped out of the car and right into her mother's eager arms.

"Oh sweetie, I'm so glad you're home," she gushed as she hugged her tightly, to the point that Bekki felt as if she might lose that cheeseburger.

"Okay, okay Ma," she laughed as she hugged her back. "I'm glad I'm home too."

Her mother pulled away and looked directly into her eyes. "Don't you dare let that dog of a man get under your skin, understand me young lady?"

Bekki felt a smile form on her lips in reaction to her mother's fierce words. "I know Mama," she promised with a sigh. Her mother had never been Mom or Mommy, she had always been Mama. It seemed unnatural to Bekki to hear her friends call their mothers by different names, but that was the way it was, growing up. Their family had always been very close and protective of each other.

"I'm so excited about you taking over the salon," her mother said swiftly to change the subject and ushered her inside to greet her father. Bekki's father was taking a tea kettle off a burner on the stove.

"Bekki," he smiled as he turned to face her. "How did you get here? Did you take the highway or the back roads?"

Bekki laughed and hugged him gently. He always wanted to know what directions she used to get anywhere, she had never really understood why, but he was determined to find the best short cuts as well as the most scenic routes.

"The highway," she replied with a smile. "I just couldn't wait to get here."

"Well, how would you like to see where you'll be sleeping?" her father suggested.

"Oh, I just thought I'd crash in my old room until I find a place," Bekki shrugged mildly.

"Hmm, I think we can do better than that," her father winked lightly and held up a set of keys.

"What's this?" she asked with surprise as she took the keys.

"Let's go for a drive," he suggested. "I want to check out your new wheels."

"Okay," Bekki replied, noticing the secretive smile he exchanged with her mother. She could tell he was up to something. She let her father drive the car and he headed straight for Rose Hill Drive.

"Oh I love this place," she sighed as the fresh air drifted in through the rolled down window and brought with it memories of travelling the streets in her teenage years. It amazed her how easily she could be transported back through time, back to adolescence when everything was of the utmost importance and yet meant absolutely nothing at the same time. When he pulled the car into the driveway of a house she glanced up at him curiously.

"Visiting a friend?" she asked as he parked the car and stepped out onto the walkway that led to the small front porch of the house.

"Welcome home, Bekki," he said as he turned back towards her and smiled.

"What do you mean?" she asked him with surprise.

"Your mother and I bought this house when the housing market crashed. It was just too good a deal to pass up. We were going to offer it to you as a..." he paused, catching himself before he finished his sentence.

"A wedding present," Bekki said quietly. "But Dad, you can't afford this," she said quickly.

"Bekki, you don't tell me what I can afford," he chuckled and gestured for her to join him on the porch. "Come on, just take a look, I think you'll like it."

"I love it," Bekki admitted as she ran her fingers along the railing of the porch. "But still, it's too much."

"Don't think of it that way," he said firmly. "It's our way of making sure that you know you always have a place to come home to. I know you might want to move back to the city, and if you do, that's okay too, you can always sell it or keep it as an investment. But as long as you are here, I want you to have this house. Make your old man smile, hmm?" he grinned and gestured to the door.

Bekki unlocked the door with a trembling hand. She was so overwhelmed and touched at the same time that she flung herself into her father's arms. He held her close and the tension in his grasp let her know that he was struggling to contain his emotions.

"I'd kill him Bekki, if I had the chance," he whispered beside her ear. "He has no idea what he's missed out on."

Bekki let a few tears slip past onto her father's shoulder, before she wiped them away and forced a smile.

"Well, give me the tour!" she requested. He happily showed her all the intricate aspects of the small house. Her parents had brought her old bed and some old furniture over already so she had some furniture to get her through until she bought some stuff. Later that day she drove her father home and shared dinner with her parents. It felt good to be home.

***

When she returned to her new house to unpack, she still couldn't believe how beautiful it was. The sun was beginning to set and the way the light played off the leaves of the surrounding trees reminded Bekki of endless summers. Bekki hefted one of the bigger boxes out of her trunk and started carrying it towards the door. The walkway was even enough but like everything else on Rose Hill Drive it was on an uphill slant. She trudged forward, the box nearly blocking her line of vision. When her foot caught on a rock that she had not seen in the walkway, she nearly lost her balance. Luckily the weight of the box was suddenly taken on by someone else.

"Whoa there, easy now," an amused voice spoke up from behind the box. Bekki caught her balance and straightened up as the box lowered and revealed a familiar face.

"Nick Malonie," she grinned as she swept her gaze over his still chiselled features. She had pined over him for months in her junior year of high school. Her heart fluttered at the sight of him and she sighed at the mention of his name. It had been a genuine head over heels crush that culminated in one very steamy summer before senior year.

"Rebekah Wilson," he replied in a formal tone and then batted one eye in a light wink. "So, the city tossed you back hmm?" he asked as he carried the box up onto the small front porch of her new home.

"Something like that," Bekki grinned.

"Their loss, our gain," he smiled warmly. Bekki felt some of her anxiety begin to ease with his kind nature. She was reminded yet again that the people of Harroway had a warm and welcoming way about them. At least, most did.

"Thanks for the help," she said as she patted the top of the box.

"Can I help with the rest?" he suggested. Bekki was a little distracted by how Nick had changed. In high school he wore his light brown hair long and flowing to his shoulders. He had a tendency to write poetry and was convinced that the world would be a much better place if everyone would listen to his favorite band. Now, his hair was cut short and neat, and his easy smile was weighted with something she couldn't quite define.

"Sure," she smiled faintly.

As they moved the boxes into the house, Nick offered casual banter about how their old high school had changed. He mentioned that the pond they had swum in had been drained and the amount of old tires they found inside of it was daunting. Bekki mostly listened. It was strange to have someone who had once meant so much to her suddenly appear in her life again. She hadn't even really thought about Nick still being in town. She had just assumed he had moved onto better things. When they carried in the last of the boxes, Bekki glanced over at Nick while he was looking over the lighting fixtures in the dining room. With his squared lips half-parted and his eyes upturned, she could easily recall that identical expression. How many nights they had looked up at the stars together. She shook her head to snap herself out of the memory.

"Let me get you some water," she smiled and walked over to the bags of groceries she had brought back to the house with her. She handed him a bottle of water and opened her own.

"It's good to see you again Bekki," he murmured before taking a swig of his water. Bekki smiled and glanced away hoping to hide how good it was for her to see him again. He stirred in her the memory that there were other men in the world, aside from Trevor. Men that she had once had amazing times with. Of course this was a different time, they had grown into very different people, but it still helped to be reminded of who she was, who Nick had been, and the poignant moments they had shared together.

"Thanks for your help," she said as she shoved the last of the boxes out of the hallway. "I hope I didn't keep you from anything too important."

"Not at all," he smiled slowly. "This is Harroway, nothing ever happens around here."

"Well, that's because they have such good law enforcement," Bekki said playfully. She had the dish about Nick's career, but had thought he had left the area.

"Oh, so you know about my badge?" Nick chuckled and actually blushed a little, as if he might be nervous about what she thought of his career.

"Sammy told me," Bekki admitted with an affectionate grimace. Sammy was her best friend throughout childhood, though they had drifted apart as adults. Sammy worked at Bekki's mother's salon.

"Ah yes, she would," Nick sighed with mock annoyance. "If it wasn't for her knowing everything about everyone in this town I might actually have to do some detective work."

"Well, I think it's great that you've achieved so much Nick, and thanks again," she walked him towards the front door of the house and he paused on the porch to glance back at her. When his green eyes met hers she recalled a kiss beneath the starlight, their first, and the way his lips had trembled with anticipation.

"Good to see you Bekki," he didn't seem to notice that he was repeating himself.

"You too," Bekki nodded cordially and waved as he walked down the walkway. She closed the door before he could look back and catch sight of her wistful smile.

"It's only memories," she warned herself as she turned to the task of unpacking. She was determined not to let herself be swept back into the arms of another man. She wanted to discover who she was, which in her current opinion, was impossible for her to do when she was wrapped up in the needs and desires of a relationship.

Still, it was nice to think of that moonlit kiss, it was something she had not thought of in years.

Chapter Two

At the salon the next day Bekki found herself in the middle of chaos. Her mother had run the business well enough but she didn't have much interest in the little aspects, like organization and finances. The salon made just enough to cover the bills and to provide an income for her mother, but it was not the finetuned machine that Bekki was used to working in. When she looked for hairspray, she found three bottles that were all on the last inch of fluid. When she sought out some fresh towels, she discovered that many of them were threadbare and thin. It was nearly impossible to figure out her mother's fee system, as she tended to charge a different rate for every customer she had.

"They pay what they can Bekki," her mother explained when she questioned her about it. "Everyone deserves to be as beautiful as she can be, regardless of how much money they can pay."

"That's sweet Ma," Bekki sighed with a shake of her head. "But it does not make good financial sense."

"Well, good thing I'm not trying to make good financial sense," her mother smiled patiently. "Bekki, things here are different than in the city. I want you to have the business, but you must not forget, this business only runs because of the people in this town, and if it were not for them, Daisy and her Curl and Coif would have shut us down long ago."

Bekki rolled her eyes at the mention of Daisy's name. She knew that her mother was right about that. Daisy had been in competition with her mother's salon since Bekki was a young girl. When she opened her salon she made a point of running an advertising campaign that painted the Wilson's salon as being outdated and incapable of keeping up with the latest styles. It had hurt the salon's business at first, but nothing could compare to the quality and skill they offered, so eventually the customers had returned to Marie's salon. Still it was not easy to deal with Daisy who was a constant thorn in her mother's side. She did her best to put down Marie's skills and to make fun of her salon.

"Don't worry Mama, I will never let that happen," Bekki said firmly.

Bekki had grown up seeing Daisy as a bully. Daisy had even encouraged her niece to pick on Bekki any chance she got. It made Bekki miserable until Sammy set her straight.

"Why would you ever care what someone else thinks of you Bekki?" her best friend had asked her. "If she knew you at all she'd love you, just like everyone else. So, don't let her get to you."

Bekki had taken that advice to heart, and had ignored the bullying until it eventually stopped.

"We do have to get things a little more straightened out though Mama," Bekki said with a sigh as she knocked over a bucket of old scissors. "It is important to be organized."

"Well, it's up to you now," her mother smiled and wiggled her fingers as she walked out of the shop. "I'm going on vacation!"

Bekki grinned and watched as her mother danced down the side walk. She was a hard working woman who had always taken care of her family in every way she could. Never once could Bekki recall her mother taking a vacation or doing much of anything for herself, but since Bekki was taking over the salon, she had made quite a few plans including travelling. Some of those plans even included Bekki's father, who was still reeling from this new independent side of his wife.

"Don't worry," Sammy assured her as she finished rinsing one of the customer's hair. "I'll help you get this place in tip top shape."

"Thanks Sammy," Bekki smiled. Her heart swelled with warmth as she felt so accepted. She wasn't missing city life at all.

***

After closing the salon that night Bekki retreated to her front porch for a little relaxation. There was enough space between her house and the street, as well as the neighbor's house, to give her some comfortable privacy. The old porch swing that hung from the wooden eaves was rickety, but held her just fine. She sighed as she began to feel the warm evening air relax her. It was like a breath along her skin as it coasted with the movement of the swing, back and forth. She took a sip of the wine she had poured for herself and briefly closed her eyes. She could recall so many memories from the sweet, moist scent of the summer evening, playing with Sammy by the creek, swinging on the tire swing on endless summer days, and sneaking out to see Nick when her parents were sound asleep... and chocolate. Chocolate? She sniffed the air slightly before her eyes fluttered open. Right before her was a tray of homemade brownies that smelled delicious.

"Just a welcome to the neighborhood," Nick offered awkwardly. "I didn't mean to disturb you," he added. He had stepped onto the porch before he realized her eyes were closed and she looked as if she was dreaming.

"Oh, thank you so much," she smiled and took a deep sniff of the brownies. "They smell delicious."

"I wasn't sure if you still liked them," he shrugged a little. They had devoured an entire tray of brownies one lazy, rainy afternoon.

"Love them," she corrected him and took one off the plate. "Have one with me?" she suggested and slid over on the swing so that he could sit down as well. He grinned and sat down beside her.

The moment he did she realized she might have made a mistake. She was so confident that she could control her feelings, as she was determined to be single, that she didn't think spending some time with Nick would bother her. But his closeness made her mind get a little fuzzy, and her heart began beating faster.

"Tell me about your job," she said quickly, hoping that conversation would break the intensity of the chemistry she was feeling. She couldn't tell if he was feeling it, too.

He finished his bite of brownie. "It's not always easy," he admitted. "I thought it would be great to have a badge and a gun, be a detective like on television," he laughed at his own youthful beliefs. "But the truth is, even though this is Harroway, I've seen some pretty terrible things."

"I'm sorry," Bekki frowned sympathetically. "I have to say though, I feel much safer knowing that you're patrolling the streets."

"Ha," he winked lightly at her. "I bet you say that to all the detectives."

"Maybe," she smiled sweetly. "But I mean it Nick, I'm sure you're a great detective. It can't be easy deciding to arrest people, knowing that they may have just made a mistake, or maybe their lives had led them to the point of making such horrible choices."

A ripple ran through Nick's jaw as he clenched it for a moment before speaking. "Actually that part of the job is pretty simple. You know some people will say that a criminal deserves to have the benefit of the doubt, but I don't see it that way. I mean, we've all had our difficulties in life, but if you commit a crime, then you should be punished."

Bekki sat back a little as she studied his passionate expression.

"Is it really always that simple Nick?" she asked quietly. After living in the city for as long as she had, she had discovered quite a few different lifestyles. Some of her closest friends had even been convicted of felonies in the past. They had made choices that weren't the best, but she didn't consider them bad people for it.

"It should be," Nick said firmly as he glanced up at her. "If the evidence is there, if the proof shows that a person has committed a crime, then it doesn't matter who it is, they get arrested."

Bekki laughed at the seriousness of his tone, hoping to lighten the mood a little.

"Hmm, I better make sure that I stay in line then," she smiled with a teasing tone. He leaned a little closer to her, meeting her gaze as he did. His nearness ignited that familiar sensation deep within her.

"So, why did you come back home Bekki? What really happened in the city?"

Bekki lowered her eyes swiftly. She took a bite of her brownie to give herself some time to choose how to answer. She wasn't quite ready to share the truth. She didn't want to admit that she had her heart broken, that she really had believed that she and Trevor were going to get married and have babies.

"I just decided I needed to get back to my roots," Bekki replied casually and leaned back against the back of the porch swing. "The city has a way of making you forget who you really are."

"But what made you realize that?" he asked, pressing for more information than she was offering, his green eyes holding a hard expression that she guessed was reserved for criminals.

"What is this, an interrogation, detective?" she laughed and then settled her lips into a smile.

"All that matters is I'm home now Nick, and that these brownies are amazing," she added and picked up another.

Nick didn't reply for a long moment as he sat back against the porch swing. She couldn't tell if he was annoyed, or just enjoying the starlight above them. She remembered that about Nick. He was always so good at being cryptic, she could never figure out exactly what he was thinking or feeling. Maybe, she thought, Trevor was the same way, maybe she had misinterpreted his coldness for being similar to Nick's thoughtful and quiet nature.

"Don't know if Harroway can handle you," he finally said with a troubled sigh. "You might turn out to be a bad influence, you know."

"Me, a bad influence?" Bekki asked with a devilish smirk as she polished off her second brownie. "Oh dear detective, I do recall some not so legal brownies..."

"Bekki!" he glared at her and then glanced around to see if anyone was walking down the street. "That was just a rumor," he hissed.

"Mmmm," Bekki grinned, enjoying teasing him. "Just a rumor."

"See I knew you'd be dangerous," he chuckled as he shook his head. "You young lady, just know a little too much."

"Maybe," she smiled lightly. "But if you keep bringing me brownies, I promise that I will keep all those secrets to myself."

"All of them?" he asked, his voice growing a little husky around the edges as he lifted his eyes back to hers. She stopped the swing suddenly by planting her feet against the wooden slats of the porch. She met his eyes boldly, feeling all of her determination flood into her expression.

"It's all in the past Nick," she promised, her words delivering a dual message that he sighed when he realized it.

"All right then," he smiled casually. "Better get back to making some more brownies," he stood up from the swing and nodded his head slightly to her.

"Good night Bekki."

"Good night Nick," she replied as casually as she could. She watched as he walked down the porch and out onto the walkway. She wondered if it was going to be a bit of a problem having him live so close by, but at the same time it actually did make her feel safe to know that he was near.

Chapter Three

When she arrived at the salon the next day she was surprised to find her mother already there.

"Mama, you're supposed to be on vacation," she reminded her with a frown.

"I know, but that Daisy has been up to no good again. I called to replenish the supplies that you needed and all of our distributors are refusing to sell to us or have raised the price."

"Why?" Bekki asked with surprise, this was certainly not how business was done in the city. "How can they do that?"

"Daisy told them the salon was changing hands and was likely going to be closed down, so now they're afraid they won't get paid," her mother lamented as she shook her head. "I don't know what that woman has against me but I wish she would just give it a rest," she sighed with frustration. "The grudges that people hold onto are just ridiculous."

When she looked back up at her daughter there were tears in her eyes. "I'm so sorry Bekki,

I wanted this to be a good thing for you, not a stressful thing."

"Don't worry about it Mama," she said firmly and scrounged up a smile. As far as she was concerned, Daisy had no idea what was about to hit her. "You just let me handle this."

She picked up her cell phone and began dialling her business contacts, then she called the distributors that had changed their prices or denied service. Once she explained the situation and dropped a few names in the industry, the distributors were more than happy to return to their previous price or offer bigger discounts. She also noticed that a lot of the customers they had scheduled for the day and the upcoming week had cancelled.

"Don't worry," she assured her mother. "They'll be back when they see what Daisy has to offer, or more importantly, what she doesn't have to offer. Now please, go home, spend some time with Dad, or go out shopping, just get this off your mind. I'm going to take care of it," she promised. Her mother was still sniffling a bit when she left the salon. The sight of her so upset left Bekki furious. She spent her entire day fuming as she thought of Daisy.

By the time the salon closed for the night Bekki was enraged. She could not believe that Daisy would sink to such a low. It wasn't the business aspect that angered her, but the fact that her mother had been sent into such a panic over everything that was happening. Determined to put an end to it once and for all she decided to pay Daisy a visit.

"Are you sure you don't want me to come with you?" Sammy offered with a frown as she watched Bekki lock the salon.

"No, I think it's better if it's just me," Bekki shook her head. "I just want to make sure she understands that I won't tolerate this kind of behavior. I'm not a kid anymore, and if she wants to fight dirty she's going to have to do it face to face."

"All right, well call me if things get out of hand," Sammy said quickly as they began to walk towards the parking lot. "I don't want anything to happen to you."

"Remember Sammy, I'm the one with the black belt," she winked at Sammy and headed for her car.

"Oh well, in that case, I don't want anything to happen to Daisy!" she shouted out with a laugh. A few customers that were still leaving the parking lot glanced up at the remark, and laughed along with Sammy. As Bekki pulled out of the parking lot she rehearsed in her mind just what she was going to say. One thing was for sure she didn't want to lose her temper. If she did Daisy would win. She was going to handle it in a businesslike fashion, at least that's what she promised herself.

***

When Bekki reached Daisy's salon she was closing as well. She had a few customers in the reception area that were settling their bills. When she saw Bekki walk in she smirked and pointed to the hours on the window.

"Sorry honey, we're closing, though it does look like an emergency," she guided her eyes over Bekki's hair critically.

Bekki rolled her eyes and folded her arms across her stomach. "I'd like to speak with you Daisy," she said firmly.

"Then speak," Daisy shrugged. "No one's stopping you."

"Okay I will," Bekki said, ignoring the customers who were now hanging around just to be nosey. "I think it's extremely immature of you to behave this way. Obviously your business isn't doing well enough to handle a little competition, otherwise you wouldn't need to cause such chaos at my salon."

"Your salon?" Daisy fired back, her eyes gleaming. "Excuse me, are you talking about that rinky dink barber shop your mother runs? That is nowhere near able to compete with my salon," she offered a disdainful laugh.

"Then you'll have no problem knowing that I have already struck an even cheaper bargain with the distributors of our products, and no matter how many customers you poach, there are many more that will come directly from your salon to ours so that someone can fix the mess that you and your stylists have made on their head," Bekki was more than fired up as she stepped closer to Daisy. "Because when you have my mother so upset, it becomes personal."

"Aw, it's not my fault your mother is so unstable, I mean, look at the man she married," Daisy offered a high pitched giggle. "It's no wonder she's so depressed."

"How dare you!" Bekki shouted and lunged towards Daisy, her instincts to protect her mother were overriding her years of discipline that karate should not be used unless it was in self-defense. The customers gasped and hurried out of the salon, while Teddy rushed in from the back office.

"What's going on here?" he asked as he got in between Bekki and Daisy. "What have you done now Daisy?" he sighed with frustration. He was obviously tired of all of the confrontations his wife caused.

"You just stay out of it," Daisy snapped and pointed her finger directly at Bekki. "You get out of my salon, and if I ever see you back here, I will make sure that you leave in handcuffs. You have no right coming over here and threatening me!"

"Oh it's not a threat," Bekki snapped back, her heart still pumping with anger. "If you do anything to harass my mother again I will be back, that's a promise."

As she turned and walked out of the salon, she heard Daisy pick up the phone and dial the police station.

"I want an officer out here right now!" she shouted into the phone. "I want to file a complaint!"

Bekki was so angry when she reached her car that she couldn't bring herself to drive. She was afraid she wouldn't pay attention to anything but her fury. All of her training was telling her that she could easily make Daisy understand what a real threat was, but she knew better. If she got herself into any serious trouble it would reflect poorly on the salon, not to mention complicate her life. But Daisy's demeaning remarks reminded her a little too much of Trevor, and touched a wound that had yet to heal. After a few minutes she finally pulled out of the parking lot.

Bekki was never someone who went to bars a lot. She did visit some clubs in New York City because that's what everyone did. It was a great way to get new customers and it also kept her up to date with the trends and interests of the younger generation. However, tonight wasn't about trends or fashion, it was about needing to calm down. She decided to stop at the only little bar in town.

There weren't too many people in the bar as it was a Thursday night, but those that were there appeared to be regulars. It seemed like a safe place to blow off some steam. As she settled in at the bar, the bar tender walked over.

"Well if it isn't Rebekah Wilson!" the man announced with surprise.

"Mr. Matthews?" Bekki replied with equal surprise. "Not teaching math anymore I see?" she laughed.

"No, I won't say that teaching school led me to drink, but it did push me into a bar!" he laughed and offered her a beer on the house. Bekki accepted it and took a big swallow of it. She began to relax as she chatted with Mr. Matthews, who insisted she call him Doug, about how the town had changed and how it had stayed the same. By her second beer most of the regulars had left and it was just her and Doug. That was when she confessed the real reason she was there, and he commiserated with her about Daisy's behavior being disruptive to the entire town. They talked for quite some time until Doug excused himself to start preparing the bar for closing, and Bekki was finishing off her beer. When the door to the bar opened, Doug called out.

"Sorry we're closing," but the two men who entered didn't listen. They just walked right up to the bar.

"Can I get a beer?" the larger of the two men asked in a gravelly voice. Bekki glanced up at him but she didn't recognize him. That didn't surprise her, since she had been gone for so long. The man that stood beside him was thinner but still quite muscular and both of them seemed to carry the air of trouble. Bekki wasn't one to make a snap judgement, but the way the larger man leaned against the bar and glared at Doug made it clear that he wasn't interested in leaving without his drink.

"I'm sorry pal, we're closing," Doug repeated and stood his ground behind the bar. While Bekki took the last swig of her drink the thinner man sidled up to her.

"Well, maybe this lovely lady will share hers," he suggested and leaned closer to her. Bekki stiffened and narrowed her eyes.

"No thanks," she replied calmly. She knew better than to engage someone she considered to be a threat.

"I wasn't really asking," he said in a slow, syrupy voice. He picked up the bottle of beer and drank the last drop. Bekki felt her heartbeat quicken as she realized that these two men had not stopped in for a drink at all. She noticed a gun tucked into the back of the larger man's pants. She started to reach for her cell phone.

"Don't do it," the skinny man warned and put his hand over hers. "Just stay calm pretty lady, you and I will have our time together soon, but first I need to take care of something."

He nodded to the larger man who withdrew his weapon and pointed it at Doug.

"Empty the register and the safe," he demanded. Doug glanced over fearfully at Bekki and then looked back at the man with the gun. "Okay, don't worry, I'll give you everything, just don't hurt anyone, okay?" he tried to stay as calm as he could.

Bekki had lowered her eyes and was pretending to be terrified. She didn't want to give the two men any idea that she had the skills she did. In truth she had only ever fought off a mugger once, but she had won plenty of competitions with much larger men, who had trained for much longer than she had. She had taken classes that involved knives, as well as guns, just in case she was ever faced with this moment. Her constant training was one of the reasons that she could eat anything she wanted. This wasn't a classroom, or a competition. Now it was real, and she felt a little nervous about whether she would truly be able to do what she intended.

As Doug began emptying the register, Bekki waited for the perfect moment. It came when the larger man with his gun in hand leaned over the top of the bar, and the skinny man glanced over at him to see what he was looking at. In that moment Bekki jumped up and shoved the skinny man into the larger man, making the two of them collide into the bar. Her eyes never left the gun, which was in the larger man's hand. As she expected him to, the larger man shoved back at the skinny man, bringing the weapon closer to Bekki as he did. Bekki seized that moment to land a blow so fierce to the man's forearm that his bone cracked. When it did, she watched his fingers spring back from the trigger and reached out with her free hand to snatch the gun from his injured grasp. Once it was in her hand, she began to hear again. She heard Doug crying out in fear, she heard the larger man scream in pain, and the skinny man begin to curse. She held the gun on both of the men, her eyes glinting as hard as rocks as she glared at them.

"On your knees," she demanded.

Doug grabbed the phone to call the police, and while he was on the phone Bekki held the two men at gunpoint.

"She's not going to shoot," one of the men said to the other. "We should make a run for it."

Bekki smirked and played her finger on the trigger. She wasn't going to let them think that she wouldn't shoot. Before she had the chance to prove it there were sirens outside. Nick and three uniformed officers burst into the bar, their guns drawn.

Nick automatically pointed his gun at the person with a weapon, and only noticed who it was after he glanced up at her face.

"Bekki drop the gun," he demanded, his voice catching in his throat slightly. Bekki lowered the gun as the other officers rushed the two men and began handcuffing them.

Nick reached out and grabbed the gun from Bekki's hand a little more roughly than he needed to.

"All right, I'm not the robber," she laughed as she looked up at him. He met her gaze with a hardened glare and she realized that he was not in the least pleased.

"What's wrong?" she asked. "How did you guys get here so fast?"

"Because," Nick replied as he handed one of the other officers the weapon and pulled out his own handcuffs. "We were looking for you."

"Me?" Bekki's heart had not slowed down yet from the confrontation with the two men. The look in Nick's eyes made it pump harder again. "Why?"

"Rebekah Wilson you're under arrest for the murder of Daisy Carmile," he spoke in a calm unwavering voice. When Bekki felt the handcuffs close over her wrists, her heart sank.

"Murder?" she gasped out. "You mean Daisy's dead?" she looked from him to Doug behind the bar, and then back to Nick. "You can't possibly think I had anything to do with it?" Her tone was incredulous as she stared at the man she had once considered the most handsome boy in class.

"I'm just doing my job, Bekki," he said through gritted teeth and led her out of the bar. He put her inside one of the patrol cars, pushing her head lightly to prevent her from hitting it on the door.

"Please Nick," she whispered as she tried to meet his eyes. "You know me, I wouldn't do this, please."

Nick studied her for a long moment, his green eyes darkened with emotion.

"I used to know you Bekki. If you didn't do this, it'll all get straightened out," he slammed the door shut. Bekki watched him walk away through the thick glass of the window.

Chapter Four

Bekki was led from the car and directly into an interrogation room. The entire time all she could think of was Daisy. Could it really be true that she was dead? She was certain that the entire matter would be cleared up easily. She sat calmly in the interrogation room, not allowing herself to panic. When the door to the room opened and Nick stepped inside she looked up at him with relief. But his expression remained hardened and focused as he sat down across from her. Behind him another detective stepped in.

"Rebekah, I'm Detective Williams," the woman said as she walked up to the table. "And this is my partner Detective Malonie."

"I know who Nick is," Bekki said quietly as she looked from one to the other. "This is all ridiculous, I mean I know you're just doing your job, but Nick do I really need to be handcuffed?" she asked with a frown.

"You two know each other?" Detective Williams said with surprise as she walked around the side of the table to unlock Bekki's handcuffs.

"We were friends in high school," Nick admitted and briefly met Bekki's eyes.

"Is that going to be an issue?" Detective Williams asked as she turned back towards Nick.

"Not at all," Nick assured her and flipped open the thin file on the table in front of him. "Rebekah, it seems that you had a confrontation with Daisy this evening," he said in a professional tone.

"Yes, I did," Bekki said feeling very flustered. "It was just a business thing."

"Really, because I have witnesses saying that you threatened her," he pointed out and met her gaze, his green eyes filled with determination. "Is it true that this is an ongoing feud between Daisy and your family?"

Bekki's mouth dropped open but she could not bring herself to speak. She was putting the pieces together much in the same way that Nick must have. She had threatened Daisy, and there were plenty of witnesses who had heard it. She could understand why it was that she would fall under some suspicion.

"Look, I was at Doug's bar all night. He'll tell you that, just ask him," she said quickly as

Detective Williams leaned against the table beside her.

"Oh, we have talked to Mr. Matthews," she said with a forced smile. "And he informed us that you had a couple of drinks, and told him how frustrated you were with Daisy. You then proceeded to pick a fight with two armed men. Did you have a few before you went to the bar Ms. Wilson?" she asked sternly.

"What?" Bekki shook her head with irritation. "Of course not. I had a couple of beers, I wasn't drunk. Was it a crime to stop a robbery?"

"It's not a crime," Nick said firmly. "But, it does demonstrate that you have the ability to attack, and obviously, you don't have a problem with physical confrontation."

"I don't have a problem with physical confrontation?" Bekki asked, her voice raising with each word she spoke. "Excuse me? So, I am trained in martial arts, that doesn't mean I would ever hurt anyone intentionally. What I did tonight was in self-defense!"

"And you broke the man's forearm," Nick clarified, his eyes locking with hers as his own voice began to rise. "Daisy had multiple contusions and broken bones Bekki, so what am I supposed to think? That you were perfectly satisfied to simply have words with Daisy and walk away, but later on the same night you decided it would be a good idea to take down two large men?" he demanded. "Obviously you were capable of the crime, and you had motive..."

"Nick," Detective Williams interrupted sharply. "Calm down," she studied him intently.

Nick fell swiftly into silence and looked quickly away. Bekki could see the ripple of his clenched jaw, she knew he could barely contain his emotions. She had a feeling though, that those emotions had less to do with anger than they did with fear.

"I'm sorry," Bekki said quietly as she stared down at the table. "I didn't do this. I didn't do it," she promised and squeezed her eyes shut for a long moment.

"Isn't it possible," Detective Williams started again in a soothing tone. "That you might have left Daisy's salon, and had a few drinks down the street at the liquor store. Then maybe, you decided to go back and finish your conversation with Daisy. When you came back, Daisy was being her usual self, and you just couldn't take it anymore. So you lost your temper, and you beat her up, maybe you didn't even realize that you killed her, and then you went to drown your anger over at Doug's bar. Don't you think that makes sense?"

"Are you insane?" Bekki snapped as she suddenly jumped up from her chair. "No it's not possible! No it doesn't make any sense! I would never kill Daisy!" she slammed her hands hard against the table, making Detective Williams and Nick jump up at the same time with the intention of restraining her. Nick glowered at her so darkly that her cheeks flushed with embarrassment.

"I'm sorry," she said and raised her hands up into the air as if surrendering. "I'm sorry," she added as she sank back down into her chair. She realized that blowing up was not exactly helping her case. "What do I need to do?" she asked in a shaking voice. "Do I need to get a lawyer?"

"I would recommend it," Detective WIlliams nodded her head as she swept the file up into her hands from the table. "I would call one fast. We don't have enough to book you tonight, but once we've done all of our interviews and we finish analyzing the forensic evidence, I can promise you Ms. Wilson we will make sure that you are behind bars. Don't even think about leaving town, understand?" she demanded.

"Of course," she muttered trying to hold back her tears. She had herself convinced that none of this would be a big deal, but now she was terrified. All of the evidence they had was true and it was stacked up pretty high against her.

"Do you want me to call Sammy?" Nick offered, his voice softening just a little when he noticed the tears in her eyes.

"Oh please, don't bother," she glared in his direction. "I think I can find my own way home."

"Bekki," Nick started to say but a look from his partner silenced him.

"We'll be in touch," Detective Williams said sternly before they both left the room. Bekki wiped her eyes and took a deep breath before following after.

***

Of course in the tiny little town word had travelled fast that not only was there an attempted robbery at Doug's Bar, but Rebekah Wilson had also been arrested. She was not feeling very proud of her choice to interfere with the robbery, even though she was certain that it had been necessary. As she walked out of the police station an old beat up station wagon pulled up at the curb.

"Need a ride jailbird?" Sammy asked as she smiled through the windshield. Bekki sighed with relief and opened the door. She settled down into the passenger seat and glanced over at her friend.

"Get me away from here," she pleaded.

"No problem," Sammy replied and drove away from the police station. "Can you believe that witch is really dead?" Sammy asked with a shake of her head.

"You heard?" Bekki asked hesitantly.

"Of course I did," Sammy frowned as she glanced over at Bekki. "I'm just sorry I didn't stick with you tonight, then we could tell all these gossips where to shove their suspicions."

"Thanks Sammy," Bekki sighed, glad that at least her friend did not suspect her.

"Are you doing okay, sweetie?" Sammy asked as she looked over at her. "I heard about you taking down those two armed men, that's amazing!"

Bekki didn't feel amazing. She felt sick in the pit of her stomach. She was scared and there wasn't much she could do about the fear she was feeling. She had a right to be scared. She might just become a convicted murderer.

"I'll just take you home," Sammy said gently in response to Bekki's silence. "I know you've had it rough tonight."

As she drove, Bekki glanced out the window. She watched all the familiar houses and buildings pass her by. The town she had once left behind for brighter and greater things, was now going to believe that she had come back a killer. Her poor parents would be shunned by the neighbors. Worst of all, Daisy really was dead. As many fights as she had with the woman, she certainly never wanted to see her dead. No one deserved to be victimized in such a way, and she could only hope that the real killer would be caught. But what if he or she wasn't? What if all this turned into her going to prison?

"I need to hire a lawyer," she murmured to herself. Unfortunately, there was only one person she knew with the connections that she needed.

***

The next morning Bekki placed the phone call.

"'lo?" was the casual response when Trevor answered the phone.

"Hey," she sighed as she tried not to let her emotions run away with her. "Listen, I need a lawyer."

"Bekki?" he asked, acting as if he wasn't sure it was her. "Are you okay?"

"I'm fine, I just got myself into a bit of a mess, and I need a lawyer."

"What kind of mess?" Trevor pressed. "Is this some kind of ploy to get back together with me?" he demanded. "I gave you the chance to apologize."

"Me apologize?" Bekki gasped out. "Oh forget it," she hung up the phone sharply and flopped back on her bed. She closed her eyes against the wave of fear and depression that threatened to settle over her. In just one day she had gone from believing her life was about to change for the better to being terrified she would never have the freedom to live it again.

"Get a hold of yourself," she told herself with a frown. "You didn't kill her, there has to be a way to prove that."

That's when Bekki decided she wasn't going to leave it in the fumbling hands of the police department, she was going to figure out who the killer was herself, no matter what it took to do so. As she sat up in her bed she recalled how it had felt when Nick had placed those handcuffs on her wrists. She was seething with anger that he would think it was acceptable to do such a thing. It didn't matter to her that it was just his job, after the summer they had shared, she expected him to know her better than that, she expected so much more from him.

She wanted to stay holed up in her house all day. She wanted to hide out from the looks and the curious questions, but she knew she couldn't. The more guilty she acted the more guilty people would believe she was. She left her house with her chin held high, hoping that no one would notice the tremble in her hands. Her mother was waiting for her at the salon.

"Oh my God Bekki, what happened?" she asked as Bekki unlocked the door. "Did you really get arrested?" she asked.

"Not exactly," Bekki replied as they stepped inside. "I was taken in for questioning, but I wasn't booked."

"Oh thank God, Dad has a call into cousin George, you know he's a lawyer," she patted Bekki's arm lightly.

"Cousin George is a paralegal," Bekki said firmly and sighed as she set her keys and purse down on the front counter of the salon. "Don't worry Ma, everything is going to be fine. I'm going to figure out who really did this."

"But how?" her mother asked, still looking very frightened. "You're not a detective."

"Well, I'm going to be one now," she replied. "Now go home and rest Ma, you're supposed to be on vacation. I have customers coming in first thing."

"Shouldn't you close down the salon for the day?" her mother suggested nervously.

"It's fine Mama," she promised. "If people don't want to come in, they will cancel their appointments." As if to punctuate this statement the phone began to ring shrilly through the salon.

"Ah there's a cancellation now," Bekki smiled grimly.

"All right if you're sure," her mother said with a frown. Just then Sammy walked in.

"Morning," she called out as she poked her head into the reception area. "Just checking to make sure there's no wild bar fight going on," she chuckled. It was Sammy's attempt to brighten the mood but it only made Bekki grimace. She didn't want to remember what she had done the night before or the way that Nick had looked at her.

After her mother left, a few customers did trickle into the shop. Some just wanted to see if they could find out more details, while others were there to show their support.

"Well, it doesn't surprise me," Mrs. Culpper said with a lofty smirk. "She had it coming, if you ask me."

"Why do you say that?" Sammy inquired as she ran a comb through Mrs. Culpper's thinning red curls.

"Well, everyone knows she had a lover," Mrs. Culpper explained in a hushed whisper. "I bet that scoundrel decided to do her in, maybe she got too old for him," she giggled devilishly.

"She was having an affair?" Sammy asked with interest and met the woman's eyes through the mirror.

"Oh yes, his name is Pete, the dry cleaner," she giggled again. "I am not sure if they were still together though. I actually saw them in the parking lot the other day having a fight. They stopped when they noticed me but I overheard something about not getting a divorce," she said in a hushed voice.

"Hmm," Sammy smiled to herself and added an extra dollop of conditioner to the woman's hair.

Mrs. Collingswood, the pastor's wife was in Bekki's chair.

"Oh dear sweetheart, I am so sorry you're going through this tough patch, but don't you worry, God always looks out for his own," she smiled sweetly at Bekki through the mirror. Bekki arched a brow and opted not to remind Mrs. Collingswood that she had not been to church in quite some time.

"I'm sure it'll be fine," she said and forced a smile.

"Well, considering all the trouble she causes, I'm just surprised she doesn't have more enemies," Mrs. Collingswood pointed out. "Do you know she even made a pass at Mr. Collingswood once? Can you believe it? A man of God?"

Bekki was surprised by that revelation. She knew that Daisy often flirted with the husbands of many of the women in town, but she had just chalked that up to Daisy's need for attention.

"I'm sorry to hear that," she said politely and began paying closer attention to what Mrs. Collingswood was saying.

"If you ask me, the police should be looking for that lover of hers. Maybe he wanted her to get a divorce and she refused. Or maybe he had a wife!" she gasped out as if she had solved the mystery right then and there.

"Maybe," Bekki agreed quietly and finished fluffing the woman's hair. "Thank you for your support Mrs. Collingswood," she smiled at the woman through the mirror.

"You have it sweetheart," she assured her. "And the support of the whole congregation."

Bekki smiled, her heart warming at the idea of a prayer circle being conducted in her honor. It was better than the image she had of the whole town pushing her out and judging her as a killer.

When their customers had left Sammy and Bekki met in the middle of the salon.

"Did you know…"

"…that Daisy had a lover," Bekki finished for her. "I heard, I wonder who he is."

"Oh I know who it is," Sammy said in a hushed tone. "His name is Pete, and he runs the dry cleaners."

"Hi Ladies," Nick said from the doorway of the salon. He tipped his head respectfully at Sammy and then locked eyes with Bekki. "Can I speak with you please?"

"Are you here to arrest me?" Bekki asked with genuine fear in her voice. Nick swept his hand over the back of his neck and gazed down at the floor for a moment in a gesture she had memorized when they were just teens.

"No, I'm not," he said dismissively and Sammy took the hint to escape through the front door of the salon. Once they were alone in the salon the silence was deafening.

"Well?" Bekki asked, a bite in her tone. "What is it? Do you want another chance to interrogate me?"

"Bekki," he breathed with frustration. "I just need some answers."

"I didn't kill anyone, how is that not answer enough?" she snapped in return and turned away from him. It had hurt her feelings to think that he would even consider the possibility that she could do something like that.

"Of course you didn't," he said flatly. "But what am I supposed to do? I have dozens of witnesses saying you were angry with Daisy, that you intended to teach her a lesson, that you even threatened her. She was killed in the time between when you left her salon and the time you arrived at Doug's bar, so you have no alibi. She called a police officer while you were in the salon, and when he arrived, she was dead."

"I don't need one," Bekki said through gritted teeth. "I didn't kill anyone. I'm sure the forensic evidence will prove it."

"So far the only thing the forensic evidence has done is ruled you in as a suspect," he shook his head as he stepped closer to her. "They found your fingerprints at the salon, and no evidence of a break in, which indicates that Daisy knew her killer. The only other prints were from her regular customers."

"Well, did you ask her lover?" Bekki asked smugly, ignoring his attempts to meet her eyes.

"Lover?" he paused as she nodded her head.

"Don't tell me a great detective like yourself hasn't figured out yet that Daisy had a lover on the side. I think that might be motive, don't you? Or do you only look at suspects that you have latent feelings for?" she challenged him and turned to face him in the same moment. He was stunned by her words, and stammered a response out.

"Bekki, that's not fair," he warned. "I didn't target you. The evidence led to you."

"Maybe, but you should know better Nick," she shook her head as she leaned against the counter of the reception desk. "How could you even suspect that I had something to do with this?"

"Well, after what you did to those two men..." he started to say.

"No," Bekki said sternly as she looked into his eyes. "You told me that you wanted to talk. I'm talking. What I want to know is, do you really think I did this?"

Nick held her gaze, his expression unflinching as he replied. "Of course not Bekki," he said quietly. "I know that you didn't kill Daisy."

"Then you can help me prove it," Bekki suggested as she stood up from the counter and stepped closer to him. "I need your resources to look into the background of a man who runs the dry cleaners in town."

"You mean Pete?" he asked calmly. "Is he Daisy's lover?"

Bekki shrugged a little. "I'm not sure, but that's what the rumor is."

"Well, you know this town and rumors," he said carefully. "Don't get too wrapped up in them Bekki."

"Oh, I think I'm wrapped up in the one that says I'm a cold blooded killer, Nick," she said and walked him to the door of the salon. "Just find out all the information you can on him, please?" she asked and met his gaze.

"I will," Nick said and started to open the door. Then he paused and looked back at her. "Bekki, I'm going to find a way to fix all of this, I promise."

Bekki was the one who was stunned as he walked out the door. His meaningful look had left her feeling that familiar flutter in her heart. Regardless of his promise, Bekki was not going to wait for him to fix things. Instead as soon as the salon was closed for the day she headed for the dry cleaner's. Unfortunately when she arrived the store was already closed. She peered through the front window hoping to spot some movement inside. As she was jiggling the lock on the door, wondering if she could sneak inside, she heard someone walking up behind her. She spun so fast that she could have easily struck out at the person who was standing just a few inches away from her. Luckily she caught herself before she did.

"No more going it alone," Sammy insisted as she stepped up beside her. "I'm going to make sure that I stick to you like glue."

"That really isn't necessary," Bekki insisted as she sighed and turned away from the shop. "It's locked anyway."

"That's okay," Sammy grinned. "I happen to know just where he goes for his dinner."

"Seriously?" Bekki shook her head in wonder. "How do you know everything that goes on in this town?"

"All a girl needs are ears to listen," Sammy smirked and offered Bekki her arm. "Nick interrupted us at the salon before I could tell you that Mrs. Culpper mentioned that she saw Daisy and Pete having a fight the other day in the parking lot," Sammy said with a satisfied grin as they walked down the street. "She overheard them say something about a divorce."

"Interesting," Bekki nodded her head and smiled, "well, that definitely makes him a prime suspect."

Chapter Five

When they arrived at the small restaurant it was not very busy. It was a little after the dinner hour and the restaurant would be closing in only an hour. Still the waitress was courteous enough to seat them.

Sammy instantly hid behind her menu and hissed to Bekki. "That's him, over there, by the window!"

Bekki glanced over at the man that Sammy was referring to. He appeared to be in his late fifties, and had thinning blonde hair sideswept across his forehead. He was dining alone from what she could tell, and didn't seem to be the least bit broken up about it.

"Bekki, don't stare!" Sammy hissed and ducked down further behind the menu. "The man could be a crazed killer, you don't want him to know that you're looking at him."

Bekki arched an eyebrow as if considering whether she did or not. However, she lifted the menu up in front of her face just before Pete glanced over in their direction. The waitress walked over to his table and refilled his soda, before heading over to take their order.

"What's good tonight Shara?" Sammy asked with a casual smile as the waitress stood with her pen poised above paper.

"Please Sammy, you know the menu doesn't ever change," she rolled her eyes and chomped down on a wad of gum. "So, what are you guys going to have?" she inquired, stealing a curious glance at Bekki.

"Just some soup and salad," Sammy requested.

"I'll have the steak," Bekki said quickly, drawing a surprised look from Sammy. "What?" Bekki frowned. "I might be dining on prison food soon, I might as well enjoy the good stuff while I can."

Sammy looked at her friend in horror, and Shara averted her eyes as if she wasn't eating up every word.

"Don't even think that way," Sammy insisted. Then a moment later she glanced up at the waitress. "In that case we'll both have chocolate milkshakes."

"Great," Bekki flashed a smile, but her attention was still focused on Pete. "Is that gentleman over there having the steak?" she asked casually.

"Pete?" Shara glanced over at him. "Oh no, he's a beef stew all the way."

"Really, not eating anything different tonight?" Bekki inquired curiously.

"Oh Pete?" Shara shrugged her shoulders mildly. "He's hungry as ever," she glanced between the two women and then lowered her voice. "I guess we all grieve just a little differently, you know."

"Oh, is he grieving?" Bekki asked as if she knew nothing about the situation.

"Well, the story goes this gal came back from New York City with a bone to pick with Daisy, she runs a salon in town. Anyway, this gal apparently offed Daisy, which is terrible enough, but poor Pete over there well, rumor is he had a thing with Daisy," she lowered her voice even further if that was possible. "Even though Daisy was married!"

"Shocking," Sammy said with an exaggerated gasp.

"Disturbing," Bekki shuddered slightly and lowered her eyes. She was glad that Shara had not recognized her, although Bekki did remember babysitting her as a kid.

"All so sad," Shara shook her head. "I mean, our town is usually so safe, too bad the riff raff always find their way in."

"Home you mean," Bekki said and locked eyes with the waitress.

"Sure, home," Shara nodded and then tapped her order pad. "I'll just get these orders in for you, back in a few minutes."

"Thanks," Sammy called out. Bekki and Sammy exchanged a long glance. So, it was not just a story about Bekki being arrested, but a certainty that she had committed the crime. That would be a lot harder to fight against, especially if the crime went all the way to court, and her fate was to be decided by a jury of her peers.

"I'm going to go talk to him," Bekki suddenly said, her heart pounding against her chest.

"What?" Sammy's eyes widened. "You can't Bekki! What if he knows who you are? What if he gets scared and decides to hurt you?"

Just as Bekki was starting to stand up, she saw Teddy walk into the restaurant. She sat down quickly and picked up the menu to hide her face. When Sammy saw Teddy she did the same.

"Oh my gosh, what is he doing here?" Sammy murmured as she ducked down further.

Teddy glanced around the restaurant a few times, as if assessing who was present, then walked slowly up to Pete's table. The men spoke too low for them to over hear their words, but their physical gestures explained a lot. Teddy paused beside the table and laid one hand on the top of it. Pete looked up at him and his ruddy cheeks went pale as he recognized the man. Teddy uttered a few calm words, though his fingertips were turning white from pressing so hard on the top of the table. Bekki braced herself, expecting a fight to break out at any moment, but instead, Pete gestured for Teddy to sit down. Teddy sat down across from the man who was known around town to be his dead wife's lover. They continued to speak quietly, their expressions not giving much away as to what they were discussing.

"Oh poor Teddy, he must not have any idea," Sammy shook her head as she glanced over at

Bekki. "Can you imagine sharing a table with the man who killed the love of your life?"

Bekki shook her head slowly. Something was not sitting right with her. She was dying to hear exactly what the two men were saying. She was just about to stand up and see if she could get a closer table, when Shara returned with their meals.

"Here you go," she smiled at each of them, as if expecting more girl talk.

"Thanks," Bekki said in a rushed voice as she tried to peer around Shara to Pete's table. By the time the waitress walked away, Teddy was gone, and Pete was picking at his food again.

"That's it," Bekki said sternly and tossed her napkin down. "I'm going to find out what they were talking about."

"No," Sammy pleaded and tried to grab Bekki's hand to stop her, but Bekki ignored her. She strode right up to Pete's table and sat down across from him. Pete's mouth dropped open, dribbling a bit of his stew from his bottom lip as he met her fierce blue eyes.

"B-bekki," he stammered. He remembered her better than she expected, which she thought was fairly odd since she could not recall their lives crossing paths too often even when she was a child.

"Pete," she replied and glanced quickly around the restaurant before leaning across the table. "I'm sorry for your loss," she said carefully, wanting to gauge his emotional reaction. His expression shifted swiftly, in such a way that she did not expect. Instead of appearing grief stricken, or even guilty, he seemed to become enraged.

"How dare you?" he shouted and shoved his chair back from the table. "How dare you sit at my table after what you did to Daisy?"

Bekki stared at him in shock and attempted to recover quickly. "I didn't do anything to Daisy," she insisted.

"Don't you lie to me!" Pete roared and soon the entire restaurant was staring at them. "I know you killed her, and I have the proof that you did!"

"I did not!" Bekki shouted back as she stood up from her chair as well, ignoring the shocked glances and gasps from the few customers and the kitchen staff. "I had nothing to do with her death. In fact, I think her lover might have had something to do with it!"

Pete glared heatedly at her as he jabbed a finger in her direction. "All right it's true, Daisy and I were lovers, there aren't too many people that don't know that. But they all know I had nothing to do with it. What I have proves it!" he declared.

"What is that?" Nick's impossibly well-timed voice called out.

Bekki turned to face him and when he glanced at her the fury in his eyes was so intense that she was silenced before she could even muster a defense.

"Show me this evidence," Nick encouraged Pete.

"Why isn't she in jail?" Pete demanded harshly. "After what she did to my poor sweet Daisy, she should be locked up!"

Nick shot a glance in Bekki's direction as if to make sure she was not going anywhere, and then returned his attention to Pete.

"Then where is the proof?" he pressed and moved closer to the irate man.

"Right here," Pete barked back and picked up his cell phone. He played a message that he received on his phone.

"Help," came the muffled voice on the message. "Help please! Bekki's gone crazy!" the high pitched squeal was full of panic. Bekki's heart stopped as she heard it. In truth it was impossible to tell if it was Daisy's voice because of all the noise and interference in the message.

"What were you doing to her?" Pete asked, his eyes gleaming. "When she left this message, were you kicking her? Were you chasing her? Did it all make you feel good Bekki?"

Bekki took a step back but before she could move another inch, Nick's hand was wound around the crook of her elbow and was holding on tightly.

"Uh uh," he said firmly as he met her eyes. "You're not going anywhere."

Bekki could feel the push of his gaze as if it had a physical force to it, before he turned it back to the people gathered in the restaurant.

"All right everyone calm down now, nothing to see here," he held out his free hand to Pete. "Give me the phone," he said sternly.

"It's my phone," Pete growled and snatched it away from Nick's reach.

"Pete," Nick warned and snapped his fingers sharply. "Give me the phone or I'll have you in cuffs for withholding evidence."

Pete narrowed his eyes and then handed over the phone reluctantly. "There just might be a few things on there that are a little personal," he said in a whisper.

Nick nodded solemnly and tucked the phone into his pocket. Without looking at Bekki, he led her out of the restaurant. Sammy came scampering behind them after throwing some cash on the table for their meal.

"I'm going to jail now, aren't I?" Bekki asked breathlessly. She had to resist every urge in her body to writhe out of his grasp. She knew that she could easily accomplish it, since she had practiced the moves so many times, but it would only lead to him drawing his weapon.

"Bekki," he growled and tightened his grasp to remind her that he knew what she had done to the two men in the bar. "Why did you talk to him about the murder?" he demanded as he finally turned to face her. Sammy skidded to a stop just behind them.

"I wanted to clear my name," Bekki said firmly and tried to meet his eyes.

"Good job," he replied shortly. "Now the entire town has heard Daisy accusing you of her murder!"

Bekki was speechless as he closed his eyes slowly and tried to restrain his temper. "If you had just done as I asked, and let me handle this, none of this would have happened."

"Really?" Bekki asked with a mild laugh as she finally found his eyes. "What difference would it have made? It won't change the voicemail, will it?"

"No," he replied as he struggled to keep his tone professional, though his face drew dangerously near to hers. "But it would have given me the chance to evaluate the evidence without everyone in that restaurant hearing it, or Pete accusing you. Which is why I asked you to let me handle it," he reminded her sternly.

Bekki tugged lightly at her arm and was surprised when Nick willingly released it.

"I couldn't just wait around to be arrested," she muttered defensively.

"Me doing my job, is not the same as you waiting around," he pointed out and shoved his hands deep into his pockets. He settled his gaze on her with one of his famous unreadable expressions and she felt as if she was a teenager again, wondering if he really liked her, or just liked her.

"Well," Bekki cleared her throat. "I can't take a chance with my freedom."

"Well, you have tonight," Nick shot back and raised a finger in the air to point directly at her. "You should be in handcuffs right now. Do you realize that?"

Bekki felt her breath grow short. She remembered her conversation with Nick on the porch, and how he had claimed he would arrest anyone that the proof led to, and yet despite the revealing voicemail, he did not appear to be reaching for his cuffs.

"Yes," she replied in a hesitant voice.

"I came here tonight to talk with Pete. It's not as if I wasn't going to investigate him, Bekki. But every time I turn around in this case, there you are, getting in the middle of things."

"I am in the middle of things!" Bekki protested as Sammy stepped up behind her. "I could not be more in the middle of things if I tried," she pointed out desperately. "Now with this voicemail, I'll just have to wait around until you show up at my door," she sighed as her words trailed off. She knew that she wasn't doing anything to help her case by getting emotional.

"Bekki," Nick reached for her arm again, this time with a gentler grasp. "It's all going to be fine. Just let me do my job, and I will make sure the truth is revealed and you don't end up behind bars."

"Forgive me if I find that hard to believe," Bekki replied quietly. "But I do recall you being the one who told me you will follow the evidence."

Nick sighed and ran his fingers back through his light brown hair before he ruffled it. "Just trust me, Bekki," he asked and tried to meet her eyes once more.

"Don't worry, I'll keep the suspect under wraps," Sammy cut in as she noticed Bekki's confidence waning. "House arrest might be for the best, hmm?" she smiled sweetly at Nick.

"That would be best," he agreed and reluctantly turned away. "I'm going to get this to the station and have it analyzed. Bekki," he called back over his shoulder without looking back. "No more playing detective!"

***

Of course the moment that Bekki arrived home, playing detective was just what she did. She sat down at her kitchen table with a pad of paper. In one column she listed the evidence that was building against her. In the other column she listed the evidence she felt she had against Pete.

"So, he's her lover," she sighed with defeat. "That really doesn't prove anything." One thing was for certain, she knew that the voicemail had to be a fake. There was no way that Daisy had been calling out her name in fear.

"He must have found someone to fake it for him," she grimaced and shook her head. It didn't matter if it was fake or not, Nick was right. She had made herself even more vulnerable by giving Pete an audience to hear his accusations and the voicemail.

There was a light knock on the front door, before it swung open. "Bekki?" her mother's voice called out from the front hall.

"Mama, I'm in the kitchen," Bekki called out. Her mother stepped into the kitchen, her eyes full of concern as she sat down at the table across from her daughter.

"How are you handling all of this?" she asked with fear causing her voice to tremble.

"Okay, I guess," Bekki sighed as she looked down at her pad of paper. "I just wish I knew a little bit more about Daisy and Pete."

"Oh," her mother sighed and leaned against the table. "That old scandal is rearing its ugly head again, huh? You know some things are better off left alone."

"What do you mean?" Bekki asked and looked up at her mother. "Do you know something about their affair?"

"Sure," she nodded slowly. "In fact, that's what probably caused all the bad blood between

Daisy and me. Me knowing, just a little too much."

"Like what?" Bekki pressed, hoping that her mother would reveal some small detail that would explain everything. "Was Pete always so violent? Was he hurting her?" she imagined an entire history of domestic violence, leading up to one culminating event.

"Pete!" she laughed and shook her head. "Oh no Pete was as sappy as they come. You see there was a time when Daisy and I were friends, not very close, but friendly enough. Just before Daisy was to be married to Teddy, she and I were sharing lunch together. As we left, Pete showed up. He declared his love for her right then and there and begged her not to marry Teddy. Daisy of course declined, and at first I thought that was all there was to it. But a few months after she and Teddy were married, I noticed Pete and her together in Pete's shop. She noticed me noticing and never spoke civilly to me again."

Bekki tapped her pen lightly on the pad of paper in front of her. "Are you saying that their affair has been going on as long as Teddy and Daisy's marriage, if not longer?" she asked with surprise.

"Well, I don't know for sure," her mother hesitated. "You know I don't like to gossip. But it seems so impossible that Pete would do something like this. I mean if they were in love for so long, what could possibly have changed? He knew about Teddy all along."

Bekki scribbled something down on her notepad and then nodded thoughtfully. "That does seem a little strange. I can't believe I never knew anything about this," she shook her head and then smiled. "I guess all little towns have their secrets. I think it's time we outed a few."

"Bekki, just be careful," her mother warned as she reached across the table to gently squeeze her hand. "I know a lot of people think the city is dangerous, but the truth is, small towns guard their secrets, sometimes even violently."

"It's okay Mama," Bekki assured her as she smiled. "I can take care of myself."

***

With Nick's words of warning ringing in her head, Bekki set off down the main street the next morning. She had two cups of coffee in her hands and positioned herself strategically in front of Pete's shop. She was determined to get some answers from him, even if it meant risking another confrontation. After what her mother had said, she was fairly certain that Pete wasn't as dangerous as he seemed. Even if he had killed Daisy, it was likely out of a moment of extreme emotion not a cold blooded act. Still she did feel a little discomfort as she anticipated the moment when he would arrive.

"Is this for me?" Nick asked as he walked up behind her and reached for the cup of coffee.

"No," Bekki said and pulled her hand back as her eyes narrowed. "Are you following me?" she demanded.

"Are you letting me do my job?" he countered as she reluctantly surrendered the cup of coffee.

"Well, maybe if you weren't so busy following me, I wouldn't have to do it for you," she pointed out in an aggravated tone.

"Nick, are you accepting bribes now?" Detective Williams asked as she joined them at the entrance of Pete's shop.

"No, of course not," Nick replied and narrowed his eyes a little at Bekki. "I just needed to speak with Bekki for a moment."

"Nick," Detective Williams warned, "she is a suspect in a murder case, even if she is your old friend. Please be careful," she eyed Bekki as if she was already a convicted criminal. Bekki offered a sweet smile in return.

"Kill them with kindness," she heard her mother mutter in the back of her head, a phrase she had heard since childhood. When Detective Williams walked away to inspect the area surrounding the dry cleaner's for any evidence, Nick turned back to Bekki and picked up right where he had left off.

"I am doing my job Bekki, I am here to conduct an interview with Pete. Alone," he added sternly.

"All right, all right, I get the hint," Bekki pushed her dark hair back over her shoulder and glanced down the street to see if Pete was on his way. "But be sure to ask him about how long his affair was with Daisy," she said quickly. "And whether he was holding a grudge against Teddy, for being the one that Daisy married."

"Bekki," Nick's voice rolled from his lips with a hint of irritation as he shook his head. "I know what questions to ask. I promise, I can actually conduct this investigation without your help."

"Of course you can," Bekki nodded quickly and then bit into her bottom lip. "But mention that Daisy must have truly been in love with him, and how it must have made him feel to not be able to be the one she married. Ask why he and Daisy were…"

"Rebekah!" Nick suddenly snapped. "Enough, I've got it," he assured her. "Now get out of here before I arrest you for obstruction."

She narrowed her eyes swiftly. "Just remember Nick, I am a black belt."

"Are you threatening a police detective?" Nick asked as he took a step closer to her, his eyes hardening back into the professional glare he preferred.

"You want to step back," an all too familiar voice shouted from a few feet behind Bekki. "Or I can report you for attempted intimidation of a suspect," Trevor suggested as he stepped up beside Bekki.

"And just who are you?" Nick asked, though his tone was fairly polite.

"I'm her lawyer," he said sternly. "And from what I understand you've made a real mess of this whole case."

"Is that so?" Nick inquired and settled his eyes on Trevor.

"Trevor, I told you not to come," Bekki sighed as she put her hands lightly on his chest and tried to steer him away from Nick. "Everything's fine now."

Nick grimaced as he witnessed the intimate way Bekki touched Trevor. He backed away from the two when he noticed Pete's car driving down the road.

"Bekki, make yourself scarce," he requested, ignoring Trevor.

"Come on Trevor, I'll buy you a coffee and explain," Bekki said and pulled him down the pavement away from Pete's shop.

"Yes, I'd love to know what's going on here. Who was that guy? Some old flame?" he chuckled darkly around his words.

"He's a police detective working on the case," Bekki sighed with exasperation. "Besides, it should make no difference to you."

"I'm here aren't I?" Trevor asked as he looked into her eyes. "You called me, said you needed help, and then I came."

"After you pointed out that I should apologize to you," Bekki reminded him with a glare. "Really, Trevor? That's a new low."

He sighed and shoved his hands into his pockets. "Do you want my help or not Bekki?"

Bekki knew that if the case proceeded she would need a good lawyer on her side. But Trevor's attitude and dismissive nature reminded her that he had never been on her side.

"No," she said strongly as she looked boldly back at him. "I don't want your help. I want you to go back to New York City, where you belong."

Trevor wiped a hand across his face and when he pulled it away he had a smirk on his lips. "Fine. Have it your way. I can see that you're exactly where you belong."

Bekki had to bite her tongue to keep from launching off a few choice words in his direction as he spun on his heel and walked away.

"Oh, is that for me?" Sammy asked cheerfully and plucked the remaining cup of coffee from Bekki's hands. "Thanks so much, it smells delicious," she paused a moment and quirked a brow as she watched Trevor walk away. "Not as delicious as he looks, however. Was that Trevor?" she gasped in a scandalous tone.

"It was," Bekki replied grimly. "He decided to pay me a visit, he graced our little town with his presence," she sighed with aggravation and shook her head slowly. "I really have no idea what I ever saw in him."

"Honestly, I don't either," Sammy replied with a frown. "In fact, I can't figure out why you haven't sealed the deal with Nick."

"Sammy!" Bekki sighed as they walked down the street together. "Nick and I are just friends. I mean, I think we're friends. We're just…"

"Old flames," Sammy supplied. "Lovers torn, a romance gone wrong…"

"Enough!" Bekki barked out and rolled her eyes. "It's nothing like that. He and I had a summer, that's it."

"The most amazing summer of your life," Sammy reminded her. "Try telling someone who wasn't there each night you cried."

"Sammy please, can we focus on the fact that I could be going to jail for murder?" Bekki pleaded and shot a demanding glare in her friend's direction.

"Oh yeah that," she laughed a little, but one look from Bekki silenced her amusement. "All I'm saying is that Nick Malonie could arrest me any time," she offered a lopsided grin and a dreamy sigh.

"I'm sure Detective Williams would love to hear about that," Bekki laughed.

"Oh yes, she does like to put a damper on things, doesn't she?" Sammy shrugged casually. "There are ways to deal with those who get in the way of true love," she grinned devilishly.

Chapter Six

Nick didn't call her until after dinner that night. When he did call, he invited himself over.

"I just want to speak to you about the interview with Pete," he explained.

"Sure," Bekki smiled a little and then wiped the expression off her face. Between her encounter with Nick's partner, and with Trevor, she was even more determined to keep her emotions and desires in check.

When he arrived she was waiting on the porch for him. He smiled at her as he ascended the steps and joined her.

"Any news?" she asked hopefully. She was ready to have the pressure of the investigation off her back.

"Not exactly," he admitted. "My partner and I did the interview with Pete, but he didn't give us too much to go on. We're still waiting for the last of the forensic evidence to clear, since everything else we have is purely circumstantial."

"Oh," Bekki frowned with disappointment as she continued to listen.

"Right now we don't have enough evidence on anyone to do anything," Nick explained diplomatically. "So, you can tell that to your lawyer," he added, his eyes gleaming slightly.

"He's not my lawyer," she admitted quietly, trying to hide the surprise in her tone at the hint of jealousy she heard in Nick's voice.

"Oh?" Nick asked as he leaned back against the front wall of the house. "Because he seemed pretty convinced that he was."

Bekki did not take the bait, and remained silent as she stared out across the front lawn.

"Is he the reason you're back here?" Nick pushed, unwilling to let the subject rest. "Some kind of history there?"

Bekki glanced over her shoulder at Nick and studied him for a moment. "Aren't you supposed to be investigating a murder?"

"I'm on a break," he replied with one of his easy smiles creeping across his lips. "So answer the question Ms. Wilson."

"We were together," she sighed as she shook her head. "At least I thought we were."

"And now?" he asked as he stepped forward, laying the palms of his hands on the back of the porch swing.

"Now I'm, home," she replied and glanced up at him so that her nose was nearly grazing his chin.

"You certainly are," Nick breathed, and then abruptly released the back of the swing. "As I said, I'll keep you up to date on any new developments, but please stay away from Pete. He is our prime suspect."

"You mean other than me?" Bekki reminded him with a playful smile.

"I mean, be careful," he warned her. He started down the steps of the front porch.

"Thanks Nick," she called out without even realizing that she intended to speak. Nick looked back at her and nodded his head slightly. Then he continued down the walkway and out to the street. Bekki watched him walk away. She couldn't believe that so many years could pass, their lives could change so much, and yet, there it was, that subtle flutter that was sure to drive her mad.

When she was sure he was gone she jumped up from the porch swing. With a quick check of her watch she knew that she was running low on time. She hurried down the steps and to her car. When she pulled off onto the street she set her cell phone on the seat beside her. When she pulled into the parking lot of Pete's shop she sent a quick message to Nick. She wasn't trying to be reckless, just thorough. She let him know where she was and what she was up to. She had Nick's number ready to dial and then she left the phone accessible in the front fold of her purse.

Pete was just getting ready to close up for the night when Bekki pushed her way confidently into the shop.

"You," he glowered in her direction. "You can't be here, you have to go."

"It's a free country," Bekki pointed out and closed the door behind her. "I believe there is something also in my rights about being able to confront my accuser."

Pete winced as he turned away from her and slapped the palm of one hand against the counter. "Bekki, I need you to leave," he warned her in a menacing tone. Bekki was not intimidated, instead she strode closer to him.

"I want to know why you faked the voicemail Pete. I know, it wasn't because you killed Daisy," she added coolly. "I know that you were in love with her. You wouldn't do that."

"No, I wouldn't," he sniffed, tears beginning to fill his eyes. "I would never do something like that to her. But it was my fault," he sighed and closed his eyes for just a moment.

"What do you mean?" Bekki asked sharply and crossed the final distance between them. Pete abruptly stood up from the counter and stepped in front of her, effectively trapping her between himself and the counter. The moment he did, Bekki slid her hand into her purse. She dialled Nick directly and left the line open.

"I mean, what does it matter who did it? If it wasn't for me she would still be alive!" he groaned and struggled not to let the tears fall from his eyes.

"Because you killed her?" Bekki prompted him. "Because she wouldn't leave her husband?"

"No! No! No!" Pete slammed his hands down on either side of the counter, his body still blocking hers. "It wasn't me!" Pete hissed as the sirens drew closer. He had Bekki pinned between the counter and the front door and he did not show any sign of moving away from her. "You have to believe me," his eyes widened. "I have an alibi, I can prove it."

"Well, then you can tell Nick all about it," Bekki said breathlessly. She wanted to subdue him, but she knew that she had already gotten herself into enough trouble with Nick. She didn't want to feel handcuffs around her wrists again.

"Nick won't listen to me Bekki," Pete's eyes were filling with panic as the police sirens pulled up in front of his store. "Listen, I had no choice. You have to believe me. It was you or it was me, he didn't give me any choice!"

Bekki stared hard at Pete, unable to fathom a single word of what he was saying. Before she could ask him to clarify, the door to the shop burst open and Nick, along with two uniformed officers and Nick's partner, Detective Williams rushed in with their weapons drawn. The moment Nick saw Bekki, she noted a flash of emotion across his expression, but to her surprise it was not the anger she expected.

"Back away from her now," Nick commanded as the other two officers continued to train their weapons on Pete. Pete raised his hands into the air and backed away slowly.

"Please Bekki, you have to believe me," he whispered as one of the officers pulled his hands firmly behind his back and cuffed him.

"Are you okay?" Nick asked as he holstered his gun and moved quickly to her side. "Did he hurt you?"

"No," Bekki replied, still trying to figure out Pete's words. "He says he's innocent," she murmured as she watched Pete led out of the shop.

"Of course he does," Nick sighed and ran his fingers across his forehead. "You know Bekki..."

"I know, I should have stayed out of it," she said, hoping to speed up the lecture.

"Yes, of course you should have," Nick all but growled. "He could be a killer Bekki, and you were here alone with him. When I got the call, you can't even imagine the things that went through my mind."

Bekki looked up into his passionate eyes with surprise. She realized the expression she had witnessed was relief. He had been worried about finding her the same way that Daisy had ended up.

"I'm sorry," she uttered gently and reached out to lightly touch his forearm. "I didn't mean to scare you."

"Didn't you?" he asked with a light chuckle. "Why else would you be running directly into danger?" he shook his head as he turned away from her. "Well, at least not much has changed. It's always me chasing you."

"Excuse me?" Bekki laughed. "I don't recall any chasing."

"Well, then you weren't paying attention," he replied casually and opened the door to the shop. Bekki stared at his back as he stepped out and onto the sidewalk. She had to gather herself for a moment before she followed after him.

"I was paying attention," she said sternly and tried to get him to turn to look at her. "What do you mean by that?"

Detective Williams shot a look of displeasure in their direction, which Nick received loud and clear.

"Now's not the time," Nick smiled tensely. "As you said before, it's all in the past."

Bekki nodded slowly. His words were the reminder she needed to keep herself on track. It was true. It was all in the past.

"You know what bugs me?" Bekki asked in a soft voice.

"What?" Nick asked without turning back.

"If Pete is the killer, then why did he plant the voicemail? I mean, why me?" she frowned.

"What do you mean?" Nick asked as he turned back to look at her.

"Well, Pete doesn't know anything about me. I'd assume he didn't know I'd returned to town, it would be a stretch to think that he was there in the salon to overhear our conversation. So why would he pick me to frame?"

Nick seemed to be considering her words as Bekki rolled over the evidence in her mind.

"Nick, you said that Daisy was killed only a short time after Daisy and I fought. When I left, Teddy was trying to calm Daisy down. So how did Teddy leave, and Pete show up within such a short span of time? Wouldn't they have had to cross paths at least to make the timeline work?"

Nick stroked his fingertips along his strong jaw line. He had been so focused on trying to prove that Bekki was not the killer he had overlooked truly paying attention to who the killer might be.

"Pete said, it was you or me Bekki," she said with a frown. "I'm not sure what that means just yet, but I know it means something."

"Are you sure you're not a detective?" Nick asked Bekki with a furrowed brow.

"Certainly not, but I can tell you this much Nick, I think you've just arrested the wrong guy."

***

Bekki paced around her living room. She couldn't sit still. She was relieved that Pete had been arrested, temporarily taking the pressure off her as a suspect, but at the same time she was puzzled. She was nearly certain that Pete had not been responsible for Daisy's death after all. However, that left her with an even more troubling question. If not Pete, then who?

"It was you or me," she repeated out loud as she continued to walk the same path along the carpet. Her mind was spinning with so many mixed emotions and thoughts that it was hard for her to clarify anything. With a heavy sigh she stepped out onto the porch. She sat down on the porch swing and stared up at the stars, hoping they would offer some kind of sign or road map as to what direction her thoughts should take. Instead they merely glistened against the passing clouds. As always the stars reminded her of Nick. It was right at the end of junior year that she had grown brave enough to approach him. When she did, she was sure that he would laugh in her face, or ignore her, but when she confessed her crush, he smiled in return. That easy smile, so languidly spreading across his lips had been the high point of her youth.

They spent the entire summer finding ways to be together. Each moment she spent with him felt so magical, so special, as if they had been the only ones in the universe to find true love. Of course she knew better now. She knew it had just been a combination of youth and hormones that made the affection they shared so intense. When summer came to an end Bekki expected their relationship to continue, but instead Nick disappeared. He was gone for two months. By the time he returned, Bekki had assumed that their relationship had just been a summer fling, and moved on with a new boyfriend. Nick never did explain to her where he had been, or why he had gone so suddenly. They spent the rest of high school ignoring and avoiding each other and then Bekki moved away.

No matter how much changed in her life, Bekki had to admit that she always fell back on those fond memories of Nick and that special summer to get her through difficult moments. They became like a fantasy to her, a place to retreat to the sweet dreams of youth, before the reality of life kicked in. Trevor had seemed so real to her, and yet in the end, he had turned out to be as fake as they come. Suddenly Bekki sat forward on the porch swing.

"That's it!" she gasped out into the night air. "It was him or me! Now I understand!"

It was late, and Bekki knew that if she called Nick with another wild idea after all of the things she had pulled lately, he would likely not believe her. She had no way to prove her theory at the moment. All she had was one very risky hunch, and a big part of her hoped that it was wrong. As she turned in for the night she hoped she had solved the mystery, and hoped that she would be able to clear her name.

First thing in the morning, Bekki was waiting beside Nick's desk. When he walked into the police station and saw her standing there, his expression was grim.

"Good morning Bekki," he said as nicely as he could.

"Guess what?" she smiled at him as she dropped a fresh cup of coffee on his desk in front of him.

"Ah," he murmured in appreciation of the scent of the coffee. He held up one finger to her as he took a small sip. Then nodded. "Okay, I'm ready," he turned his full attention on her.

"I solved the case," she smirked and rapped her knuckles lightly against his desk.

"Oh really?" he laughed out loud, drawing the attention of some of the other officers in the station. "And just how did you do that?"

Bekki considered how to answer that question. She really didn't want to detail how their fling several years before had reminded her that it wouldn't matter what he did, she would never do anything to hurt him. She had the feeling that Pete felt the same way about Daisy.

"Let's just say, I'm trusting my instincts," she said secretively. "But more important is the fact that you have the wrong man in jail."

"I do not," Nick countered, his lashes tightening around his green eyes.

"You do too," she replied sharply and narrowed her own eyes in response.

"No, I don't," he insisted and stood up from his desk.

"But, I'm telling you, Pete is not the murderer," she said, her voice raising an octave.

"I know," Nick smiled.

"I mean it," Bekki started to say, and then stopped. "Wait, you know?" she asked with surprise.

"Yes, Pete had an alibi. He was with a late customer when Daisy was killed. So there is no way he is the killer. Which unfortunately returns you to our prime suspect position," he said with a grimace. "You really have to stop investigating on your own, you're getting me into serious trouble with my partner. She already thinks I'm offering you special favors since we know each other."

"Are you?" Bekki asked curiously. When Nick avoided looking directly at her, she knew that he wasn't going to answer honestly.

"Of course not," he said firmly. "But we both know that you didn't kill anyone Bekki. We just have to find a way to prove that."

"Well, it's a good thing I solved the crime then," she said quickly, her eyes shimmering with the anticipation of sharing the truth with him.

"Bekki," Nick shook his head and smiled faintly as if he did not know where to begin with her. "I can't wait to hear this."

"You will hear it," Bekki insisted with a mischievious smile. "Just follow my lead."

"Always chasing," he mumbled under his breath as Bekki led him out of the police station.

***

About an hour later Bekki arrived at Daisy's salon. Teddy was inside sorting through some of the paperwork.

"Hi Teddy," Bekki said softly as she let herself in. Teddy looked up at her, startled.

"Bekki, what are you doing here?" he asked with a grimace.

"I just wanted to check on you," Bekki murmured and let the door fall shut behind her.

"Bekki I really don't think it's a good idea for you to be here," Teddy said apologetically as he stood up from behind the reception desk.

"Teddy, you and I both know that I didn't kill Daisy," she said firmly. "I just wanted to thank you for standing up for me that night, with Daisy. I meant to thank you then, but it slipped my mind."

"Well, Daisy could get a little out of hand," Teddy admitted with a sigh. "I have no idea who killed her Bekki, but you did have an argument with her that night."

Bekki nodded and leaned against the desk beside him. "As I recall you and Daisy had a few words that night as well. Did you fight often?"

Teddy frowned as he shuffled the papers in his hands. "We'd been married for a long time Bekki, arguments were bound to happen."

Bekki nodded slowly. "You must miss her so much," she continued, easing further into the conversation.

"I still can't believe it," he murmured, his voice strangled by grief as he rested his head in his hands. "She's gone."

"I'm sorry Teddy," Bekki said with genuine sympathy. "I know that losing someone you love can be the worst feeling that you ever experience."

"It is," he agreed and looked up at her with tears in his eyes. "I'm sorry you got mixed up in all of this Bekki."

"Can it really be your fault?" she asked in a gentle tone. "Really the fault lies with Daisy and Pete, doesn't it?"

Teddy stared at her, stunned by her words. "What are you saying?" he asked, and swallowed thickly.

"After so many years of marriage, after you had been so loyal to her, to find out about them, had to be the harshest experience."

Teddy hung his head. "I had no idea that Daisy was with Pete. I only suspected when I found the deed to the Dry Cleaners in her papers. She was a joint owner with Pete. I can't believe all those years of marriage led to this," his voice raised with anger over his last words.

"I know that must have hurt you," Bekki assured him and took one of his hands in hers. "You did so much for Daisy, and treated her with so much love. To find out she betrayed you must have really pushed you over the edge."

"It did," he admitted, his words torn by a sob.

"And when she didn't even deny it," Bekki murmured, making sure her voice was loud enough for the microphone to record. "All of that anger you must have felt."

"She laughed in my face," he gasped out, and then suddenly his face went pale. "I mean, I didn't mean to say that!"

Bekki met his gaze sternly. "Calm down Teddy. Everyone will understand why you did what you did. Daisy was horrible to everyone, worst of all you. She trampled all over your heart, how could you not react when she told you the truth?"

"No," he shook his head firmly. "No, I wouldn't do that to her!"

"Of course you wouldn't. Not on purpose," Bekki prompted him gently. "But when that anger came over you, you couldn't control yourself, could you?"

"No," he wept and laid his head back into his hands. "I couldn't stop myself. She just wouldn't stop laughing at me. Oh what have I done? "

"So, you blackmailed Pete to help you frame me or he would have lost half the dry cleaners?" Bekki questioned.

"I am so sorry Bekki," he wept.

Bekki sat back slowly as she heard the door open to the salon. She heard the footsteps of the police officers approaching. As she watched Teddy being led away in handcuffs she couldn't help but feel some sympathy for him. He had discovered that his entire marriage was a lie. It had been devastating for Bekki when she found out about Trevor cheating on her, and that was only after two years. Daisy and Teddy had been married for at least thirty.

Bekki felt warm hands slide down over the curve of her shoulders followed by a gentle squeeze.

"Are you okay?" Nick asked gently.

"I think so," Bekki sniffed and wiped at her eyes.

"What you said in there, about knowing how it feels to lose someone you love," he paused a moment, his voice barely above a whisper. "That was about Trevor wasn't it? Did he break your heart?"

Bekki stared up at him, her lips dangerously close to his. "No," she shook her head slowly. "It wasn't about Trevor."

Nick's eyes widened slightly but his next question was lost on the tip of his tongue. "You did good work Bekki," he finally said, reluctantly changing the subject as he knew it was not the time or place to hash out their past.

"At least we finally know the truth," Bekki sighed with relief. "No matter how sad it may be."

Nick nodded as he helped her up from her chair. "Thanks to you, Bekki. You helped us figure it out."

"So, maybe I'm not a bad influence after all?" Bekki asked, her lips curving upward into a mild smile.

"I wouldn't go that far, just yet," he grinned, and they walked out of the salon together.

The End

More Cozy Mysteries by Cindy Bell

Heavenly Highland Inn Cozy Mystery Series

Murdering the Roses (Heavenly Highland Inn Cozy Mystery 1)

Bekki the Beautician Cozy Mystery Series

A Dyed Blonde and a Dead Body (Bekki the Beautician Cozy Mystery 2)

Mascara and Murder (Bekki the Beautician Cozy Mystery 3)

Pageant and Poison (Bekki the Beautician Cozy Mystery 4)

Made in the USA
Las Vegas, NV
08 June 2023